Contents

Oscar's brother
Focus: o as in *son*, **-ve** as in *love*.................... 3

The big pull
Focus: oo, **u** as in *book, put*.......................... 5

Nick's noisy new toy
Focus on: oy, **oi** as in *boy, coin* 18

Phonemes: ch, sh, th, wh, ph, a_e, ai, ay, e_e, ea, ee, y *as e*, i_e, ie, igh, y *as i,* o_e, oa, ow, u_e, ue, oo, ew, ar, or, er, ir, ur, wr, <mark>-ve, o, oo, u, oy, oi</mark>

'Tricky' words: my, can't, does, love, here, are, look, our, eyes, house, were, <mark>little</mark>

About this book

These short stories are designed to give children blending and reading practice. They are decodable, which means the words in them only include letter shapes and sounds that the children have learned. The stories gradually introduce 'tricky' words, building on the learning in the Red Series.

The progression links directly to the teaching order in the Letterland teaching range. Each story begins with a title page that provides important information for children and teachers.

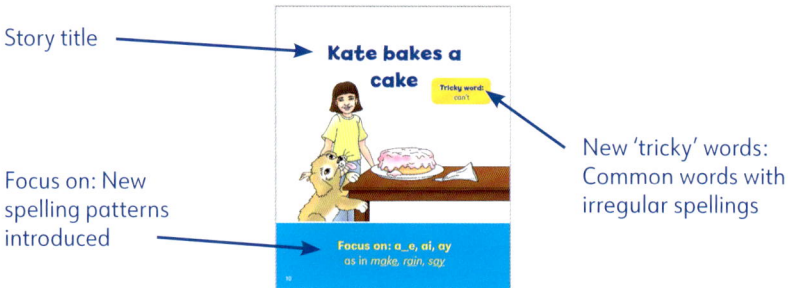

Story title

Focus on: New spelling patterns introduced

New 'tricky' words: Common words with irregular spellings

Basic teaching tips:

- Encourage the sounding out of decodable words (and any decodable parts of 'tricky' words).
- Discuss the stories with the children to ensure comprehension and engagement.
- Encourage re-reading in pairs or individually to develop fluency and reading for meaning.

Red Series introduces the a-z letters and sounds and some 'tricky words'. On completion of this series, the following words remain tricky in part: a, the, she, oh, for, that, ok, they, says, her, this, to, said, of, what, you, was, want, come, sees, asks, do. These words are included in **Blue Series**.

Oscar's brother

Tricky word: little

Focus on: o, -ve as in *s_on_, lo_ve_*

Meet Oscar's Bothersome Little Brother

He's just a baby and he can't say 'o'. So...
'uh,' he says in l_o_ve, 'uh,' he says in gl_o_ve,
'uh,' he says in s_o_n, 'uh,' he says in d_o_ne.
Is he d_o_ne saying, 'uh'? No, there are _o_thers...
What a Bothers_o_me Little Br_o_ther!

The big pull

Focus on: oo, **u** as in *b<u>oo</u>k*, *p<u>u</u>t*

Clever Cat stood in her kitchen looking at her cookbook. She spotted a good cake.

"Carrot cake," she said. "Let's see what I need: carrots... hmm. I think I have carrots."

She went to look. She pushed things here and there. She looked on the top shelf. She looked on the bottom shelf.

"Oh, no. There are no carrots!" She stood up.

"I think there may be a carrot left growing in my garden."
 It was a cool day. She took her wool cape off the hook. She put it on, then went to her garden.

"Yes, here is that carrot. I'll just give it a pull and soon I'll be making carrot cakes."

Clever Cat pulled, and then she pulled harder, but the carrot was stuck.

Just then, Peter Puppy came along the path from the pine woods. Clever Cat told him the carrot was stuck. Peter understood and said, "We can pull it together."

So Clever Cat pulled on the carrot. And Peter Puppy pulled on Clever Cat. They both pulled and pulled, but the carrot was stuck.

"We need more help," said Peter.

Just then, Ben came along.
"I'll put my big, bunny foot on the right and my other foot on the left. We can pull it together," said Ben.

So Clever Cat pulled on the carrot. Peter Puppy pulled on Clever Cat and Ben pulled on Peter Puppy.

But that carrot did not come up!

Then Oscar came along with his Bothersome Little Brother. Oscar wanted to help, too.

So Clever Cat pulled the carrot. Peter pulled Clever Cat. Ben pulled Peter. And Oscar pulled on Ben. But that big carrot was still stuck!

Then, Oscar's Little Brother said, "Uh, uh, uh."

"He wants to help," said Oscar. "But he's too tiny."

"Well, we might as well let him try," said Clever Cat.

So then, Clever Cat pulled on the carrot. Peter Puppy pulled on Clever Cat. Ben pulled on Peter. Oscar Orange pulled on Ben.

And... Oscar's Little Brother pulled on Oscar.

Out came THE BIGGEST CARROT EVER!

They helped Clever Cat make carrot cake.
It was so good and they ate lots!

Nick's noisy new toy

Focus on: oy, **oi** as in *b**oy**, c**oi**n*

Noisy Nick has a new toy robot. It has joints and hands that can pick up coins!

It makes lots of noise, too. It makes a, "rrrrr" noise when it speeds along and it beeps!

Nick makes a stack of blocks. He points the robot at the stack. The robot smashes into the stack! Crash! Nick loves the noise.

Just then Nick's Dad comes in. "Dad," said Nick, "my robot can destroy block stacks!"

"Fantastic," Dad said. "But please take that noisy toy to Roy's. He will enjoy it."

Nick put the toy in its box so he didn't spoil it.

Nick went to Roy's. "I have a new toy," he said to Roy.

"I have a new toy, too," said Roy.

Both boxes started making noises, "Beep, beep, rrrrrr, rrrrrr, beep!"

"This is fun!" said Roy.

"YES! NOISY FUN!" Noisy Nick yelled.

About this series

This series of 10 books accompanies the Letterland teaching range. Each book contains a selection of short stories. In total there are 32 engaging stories featuring the phonic elements listed below as well as some 'tricky' high-frequency words.

Book	Focus elements	As in the word...	Story titles
1	sh, ch, th, th, wh, ph	chip, shop, that, thing	Check on the chicks Shep and me What is that thing?
2	a_e, ai, ay	make, rain, say,	A safe place Kate bakes a cake Kane's tail!
3	e_e, ea, ee, y	these, sea, bee, baby	A trip to the sea Mr E's trees Happy!
4	i_e, ie, igh, y	like, tie, night, my	Ben rides his bike Cats at night What a mess!
5	o_e, oa, ow	home, boat, show	The bad goat When the cold wind blows Lost in the Queen's maze
6	u_e, ue, oo, ew	cube, blue, moon, few, grew	Stuck on a dune A day at the zoo The Hat Man's new roof
7	ar, or, er, ir, ur, wr	farm, for, her, girl, fur, write	The big match Snapshots The bird girls My very bad morning
8	o, oo, u, oy, oi	son, book, put, boy, coin	Oscar's brother The big pull Nick's noisy new toy
9	aw, au, ow, ou	saw, cause, how, out,	Draw it! The house mouse Look now!
10	Review ear, air	pear, year, fair	My shark dream A fresh feast Bears at the fair A fairy story

23

Collect the sets

Phonics Readers - Red Series

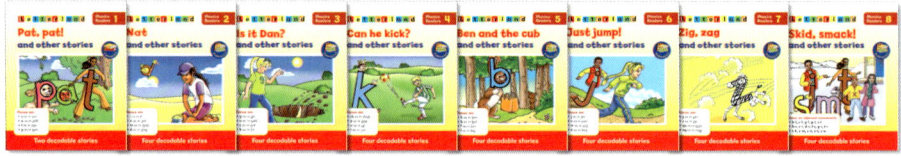

Phonics Readers - Blue Series

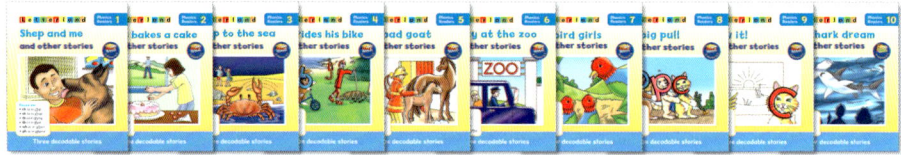

Published by Letterland International Ltd. 8/10 South Street, Epsom, Surrey, KT18 7PF, UK.
www.letterland.com
ISBN: 978-1-78248-187-4
Product Code: TJ09

© Letterland International 2016
LETTERLAND™ is a trademark of Letterland International Ltd.

First published 2013. This new edition published 2016.
Reprinted 2023.
10 9 8 7 6 5 4 3 2

Author: Stamey Carter and Lisa Holt
Originator of Letterland: Lyn Wendon
Artwork: Baz Rowell
Design: Lisa Holt

The author asserts the moral right to be identified as the author of this work. All rights reserved. No part of this publication may be reproduced, stored in a retrieval system, or transmitted in any form or by any means, electronic, mechanical, photocopying, recording or otherwise, without either the prior permission of the Publisher or a licence permitting restricted copying in the United Kingdom issued by the Copyright Licensing Agency Ltd, 90 Tottenham Court Road, London W1T 4LP. This book is sold subject to the condition that it shall not by way of trade or otherwise be lent, hired out or otherwise circulated without the Publisher's prior consent.

Printed in Beirut, Lebanon.